April 26, 1996

Happy Birthday, Mom!

Happy Birthday, Dolores!

I hope that this brings to your belly a smile to your face!

Love,
Barbara

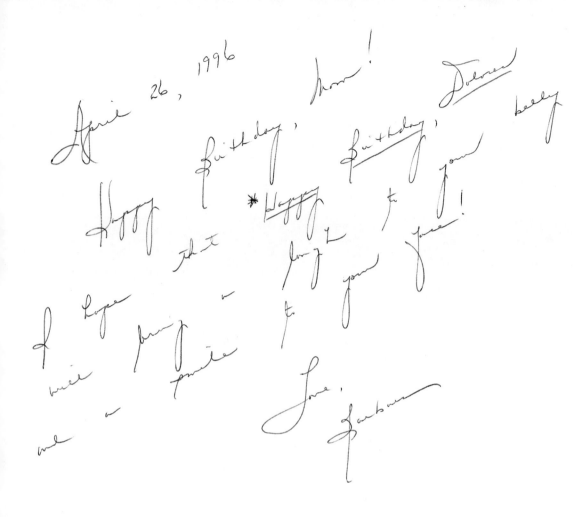

HAPPY BIRTHDAY, DOLORES

BY BARBARA SAMUELS

ORCHARD BOOKS

A DIVISION OF FRANKLIN WATTS, INC.

NEW YORK

Thanks to Hester Ward for her artistic inspiration.

Orchard Books
A division of Franklin Watts, Inc.
387 Park Avenue South, New York, New York 10016

Orchard Books Canada, 20 Torbay Road, Markham, Ontario 23P 1G6

The text of this book is set in 14 point Aster.
The illustrations are watercolors with a fine black line which were
reproduced in full-color.
Manufactured in the United States of America
Book design by Sylvia Frezzolini

10 9 8 7 6 5 4 3 2 1

Library of Congress Cataloging-in-Publication Data
Samuels, Barbara.   Happy birthday, Dolores/by Barbara Samuels.
p.   cm.   Summary: Dolores has a birthday party which is extremely
boisterous but quite enjoyable.
ISBN 0-531-05791-7.   ISBN 0-531-08391-8 (lib. bdg.)
[1. Parties—Fiction. 2. Birthdays—Fiction.]   I. Title.
PZ7.S1925Hap   1989   88-15469
[E]—dc19   CIP
                                                                                  AC

To
DANNY, JOSHIE,
and MEREDITH

One day Dolores woke up
earlier than usual.

She took a long bath,   sprinkled herself with powder,

and borrowed her sister Faye's   brand-new hot-pink nail polish.

Then she put on her favorite outfit. "Wouldn't you look nice in your new blue party dress?" said her mother.

"No," said Dolores, but she agreed to take off her helmet, cape, and boots.

"Come to the kitchen," said her mother, "and we'll decorate the cake."

"What this cake needs," said Dolores, "is a picture of my cat, Duncan," and she made one out of colored frosting.

"I think it's dumb to put Duncan's picture on a birthday cake," muttered Faye.

"It's my cake, so buzz off!" said Dolores.

"Daddy," said Dolores,
"I'm going to win all the
games and keep the prizes!"

"But Dolores, you are the hostess and the hostess can't win any prizes."

"Can't the hostess win just one very teeny little prize?" she asked.

"Well...maybe just one,"
said her father.

"Being the hostess isn't easy," said Dolores. "I have to lay out all the place cards so Stewie won't sit next to me. HE DRIVES ME CRAZY!"

"Then I must hide Duncan in the closet. Little children can be very rough with animals."

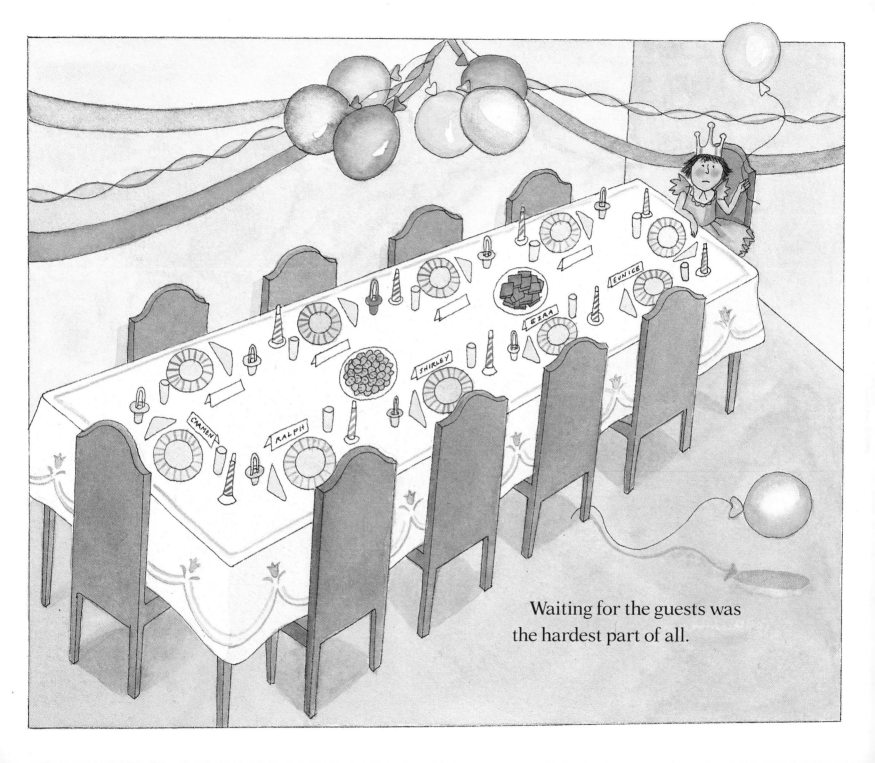

Waiting for the guests was
the hardest part of all.

When all the guests had arrived, Hal the Magician began the magic show. Every time he did a trick, Stewie yelled out, "I've seen that one a billion times!"

Finally, Dolores shouted, "If you're so smart why don't you try it!"

"Dolores dear," said her mother, "why don't you pass out the spoons for the potato race."

Stewie won the potato race

and musical chairs

and pin-the-tail-on-the-donkey.

"I didn't win any prizes," said Dolores, "but it's my birthday, and I get all the presents."

"Oh boy, a Talking-Beanie-Bunny!"

"Oh dear, two Talking-Beanie-Bunnies!"

"Oh no, three Talking-Beanie-Bunnies!"

Then her mother whispered
something in her ear.

"Thank you," said Dolores, "I can always
use more than one Talking-Beanie-Bunny."

It was almost time to eat. The guests were getting restless.

Faye showed them
how to play statues.

Stewie froze for
almost three minutes.

"Time to eat," said Dolores's mother. "Come and get it." But nobody did because just at that moment...

Arthur and Eunice found Duncan.

Everyone wanted to pet him...

but he ran away.

So they all tried
to catch him...

"HOT DIGGITY!" said Stewie,
"a birthday pizza. I'll have
chocolate ice cream on mine!"

But first everyone sang
"Happy Birthday, Dolores,"
and then, when it was very
quiet, she made a wish.

Later that night Dolores told
her mother her birthday wish.

"I wished it was my birthday tomorrow,
and the next day, and the next,
and the next, and the next..."
and then she fell asleep.